WORDS IN MY WORLD

The I Can Look It Up Book

Written by Yvonne Russell

Illustrated by Dennis Hockerman

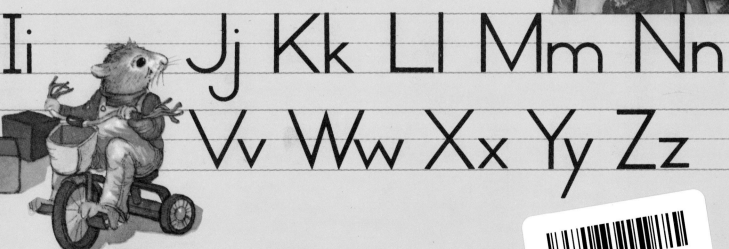

I i   J j K k L l M m N n

V v W w X x Y y Z z

Copyright © 1979 Rand McNally & Company
All rights reserved
Printed in the United States of America
by Rand McNally & Company

Library of Congress Cataloging in Publication Data

Russell, Yvonne.
  Words in my world.

  SUMMARY: Contains illustrated lists of words grouped
according to such topics as parts of the body and fruits
and vegetables.
  1. Spellers. 2. Vocabulary — Juvenile literature.
[1. Spellers. 2. Vocabulary] I. Hockerman, Dennis. II. Title.
PE1145.2.R8   428'.1   79-17654
ISBN 0-528-82090-7

A Word to Parents

"How do you spell hippopotamus?"
"How do you spell wrench?"
"How do you spell zoo . . . table . . . garage?"
The plaintive refrain "How do you spell . . . " is heard through the house when your child begins the magic process of decoding and controlling words on paper. The question may produce mixed feelings — pride in the child who tries, but frustration, too, after you have absentmindedly, and slowly, repetitiously, spelled the twenty-fifth word while trying to balance the checkbook or prepare dinner for eight by six o' clock.

WORDS IN MY WORLD is intended to ease that frustration. The more than 300 words selected for illustration are those commonly found in today's child's environment. They are gathered in recognizable groups. Zoo words are together, as are farm words, things that go, furniture, and that brand-new category — space. The words are shown in an action-crammed illustration. Beside the large picture, key words are picked out and illustrated in isolation, the better to be seen by the child. The words themselves appear in the manuscript printing favored by early-grade teachers.

WORDS IN MY WORLD is particularly designed for the child to use without adult assistance. With that in mind, go through the book once with the child. Enjoy the illustrations. Point out the illustrated table of contents with its groupings of words.

Turn to this or that desired group to find a favorite word or two. You might even point out, for the older child, the alphabetical listing of the words on the page — using the book as a pre-dictionary. In time you will sit back, balance your checkbook, or prepare company dinner, and hear your child say, "I can look it up myself!" — a satisfying moment for both of you.

I'd like to dedicate this book to John, Scott, and Mark, my three "inspirations."

Yvonne Russell

Where Things Are

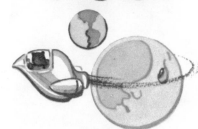

Me

 arms   legs

 elbow   foot

 fingers   knee

hand   toes

 body

 face

ear

 eye

 hair

mouth

 nose

 teeth

"Teacher,
how do you spell
bubble gum?"

girl

boy

teacher

9

Family and Friends

 baby

 brother

 doctor

 father

 fire fighter

 grandfather

 grandmother

 hard hat

10

mail carrier   sailor

 mother   sister

 nurse   soldier

 police officer   vendor

"Hilary, how do you spell crowded?"

"Walter, how do you spell trouble?"

A House

bricks

chimney

door

downspout

driveway

fence

garage

gate

grass

gutter

mailbox

porch

roof

sidewalk

window

yard

13

Inside a House

 attic

 basement

 bathroom

 bedroom

 dining room

 family room

 kitchen

 laundry room

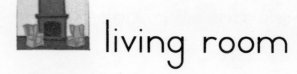 living room

 workshop

"Operator, how do you spell busy?"

Furniture

 bed

 bookcase

 chair

 chest

 clock

 lamp

 mirror

 piano

 record player

 refrigerator

 rug

 sofa

 stove

 table

 telephone

 television

17

Working with Tools

crowbar

drill

engine

hammer

hose

ladder

 pulley

saw

sawhorse

screwdriver

squeegee

wheelbarrow

"Priscilla, how do you spell wobble?"

 jack

pliers

 workbench

wrench

Playthings

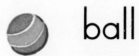 ball

 blocks

 clay

 crayons

 doll

 glue

 paint

 paper

 puppet

 puzzle

 roller skates

 scissors

 tape

 teddy bear

 tricycle

 wagon

"Ernie, how do you spell sticky?"

20

PUPPET THEATER

"Hedda, how do you spell ripped?"

Clothing

belt

boots

coat

dress

hair ribbons

hat

jacket

jeans

mittens

pajamas

purse

shirt

shoes

skirt

socks

sweater

23

Things to Eat

 bread   cookies   ice cream

 butter   eggs   juice

 cereal   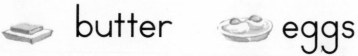 hamburger    milk

 cheese   hot dog    pie

"Mabel, how do you spell tasty?"

salad

soup

spaghetti

steak

25

Fruits and Vegetables

- apple
- banana
- beans
- carrot
- celery
- corn
- cucumber
- grapes
- lemon

- lettuce
- orange
- peas
- pineapple
- potato
- pumpkin
- squash
- tomato
- watermelon

"Irma, how do you spell crash?"

26

Buildings

church

factory

department store

 fire station

"Oscar, how do you spell scurry?"

MAYOR'S MODEL CITY

 gas station

 police station

 hospital

 school

Things that Go

 airplane

 bicycle

 boat

 car

 fire engine

 helicopter

 skateboard   train

 tractor   truck

"Rocky, how do you spell dizzy?"

A Playground

chin-up bar

drinking fountain

fort

merry-go-round

monkey bars

pole

sandbox

seesaw

slide

soccer ball

steps

swing

tetherball

tunnel

The Zoo

alligator   deer

bear   elephant

camel   giraffe

gorilla

hippopotamus

kangaroo

lion

monkey

rhinoceros

seal

tiger

wolf

zebra

"Mama, how do you spell balloon?"

35

Farm Animals

calf

cat

chicken

colt

cow

dog

donkey

duck

goat

goose

horse

lamb

pig

rooster

sheep

turkey

"Wilbur, how do you spell square dance?"

37

"Wanda, how do you spell burnt?"

The Countryside

barn

bush

cloud

field

flowers

haystacks

hills

lake

mountains

orchard

river

road

 rocks   waterfall

 tree   windmill   39

JOHNSTON
BRUSH CO.

Woodland Animals

bird

butterfly

chipmunk

fox

frog

mouse

rabbit

raccoon

skunk

snail

snake

squirrel

"Spencer, how do you spell song?"

owl

porcupine

turtle

worm

41

Space

 antenna

 astronaut

 computer

 Earth

 fuel gauge

 helmet

 moon

 planet

 robot

 rocket

 satellite

 shuttle

 space probe

 spaceship

 spacesuit

 star

"Hermoid, how do you spell aliens?"

Numbers and Colors

 black

 blue

 brown

 green

 orange

 red

 pink

 purple

 yellow

 white

1 one

2 two

3 three

4 four

5 five

6 six

7 seven

8 eight

9 nine

10 ten

"Ruby, how do you spell hang on?"

44